The Princess and the Frog

Collect all the books in the series:

The Three Billy Goats Gruff

The Three Bears and Goldilocks

The Ugly Duckling

Little Red Riding Hood

The Story of Rumpelstiltskin

First published in Great Britain by HarperCollins Publishers Ltd in 1992
First published in this edition in Picture Lions in 1997
1 3 5 7 9 10 8 6 4 2
Picture Lions is an imprint of the Children's Division, part of HarperCollins Publishers Ltd,
77-85 Fulham Palace Road, Hammersmith, London W6 8JB.

ISBN: 0 00 664647 6

Printed and bound in Singapore.

The Princess and the Frog

Retold & Illustrated By

Jonathan Langley

PictureLions
An Imprint of HarperCollins*Publishers*

Once upon a time, long ago, when the world was not as it always has been and rivers flowed uphill as well as down, there lived a king who had seven daughters. The six elder daughters had each gone to seek their way in the world, only Ivy, the youngest daughter, still lived at home.

Ivy was not like her older sisters, who were very fine and sensible and enjoyed doing royal things such as wearing crowns and going to grand balls. Ivy was happiest playing in the fields and woods that surrounded her father's castle. She especially liked to play with the beautiful, shiny, golden ball which her father had given her. It was the most treasured of all her possessions.

One bright sunny morning Ivy gulped down her breakfast, then ran out of the castle and into the fields, kicking her golden ball ahead of her. She ran across one field, then another, until she reached the edge of the big wood where she kicked the ball as hard as she could. Ivy watched as it rose high in the air, over the top of some smaller trees, then down through the branches of a tall oak until it fell - SPLASH! - into the middle of a deep pool where it sank out of sight.

Quickly Ivy found a long stick and prodded around in the pool, but she couldn't feel the ball anywhere and all she fished out was mud and weed.

Ivy was feeling desperate and began to cry.

"BOO HOO HOO!" she wailed and sobbed.

Then she heard a voice saying, "Princess, why are you crying?" Ivy looked around to see where the voice was coming from. All she could see was a green frog sitting on a rock by the pool.

"Did you say something?" said Ivy.

"Yes," said the frog. "What has made you so upset?"

"My beautiful golden ball has fallen into the pool and I can't get it out," said Ivy. "The water is so deep and I can't swim... BOO HOO HOO!"

"Don't cry," said the frog. "I can find your ball. But what will you give me if I do?"

"I will give you anything you want," said Ivy. "You can have my jewels, my fancy royal clothes, even my best crown, if only you will find my golden ball."

"I do not want your jewels or your clothes or even your golden crown. I want to be your friend. I want to sit beside you at the table, eat from your golden plate and drink from your golden cup. I want to sleep on a silk cushion beside your pretty bed. And I want you to kiss me goodnight before you sleep. If you promise me these things," said the frog, "I will find your golden ball."

Ivy thought the frog was talking a lot of nonsense but she wanted her golden ball so much she was willing to agree to anything.

"I promise all you ask," she said, "if only you will find my golden ball."

The frog smiled and said, "Remember, you've promised." Then he dived down deep into the pool.

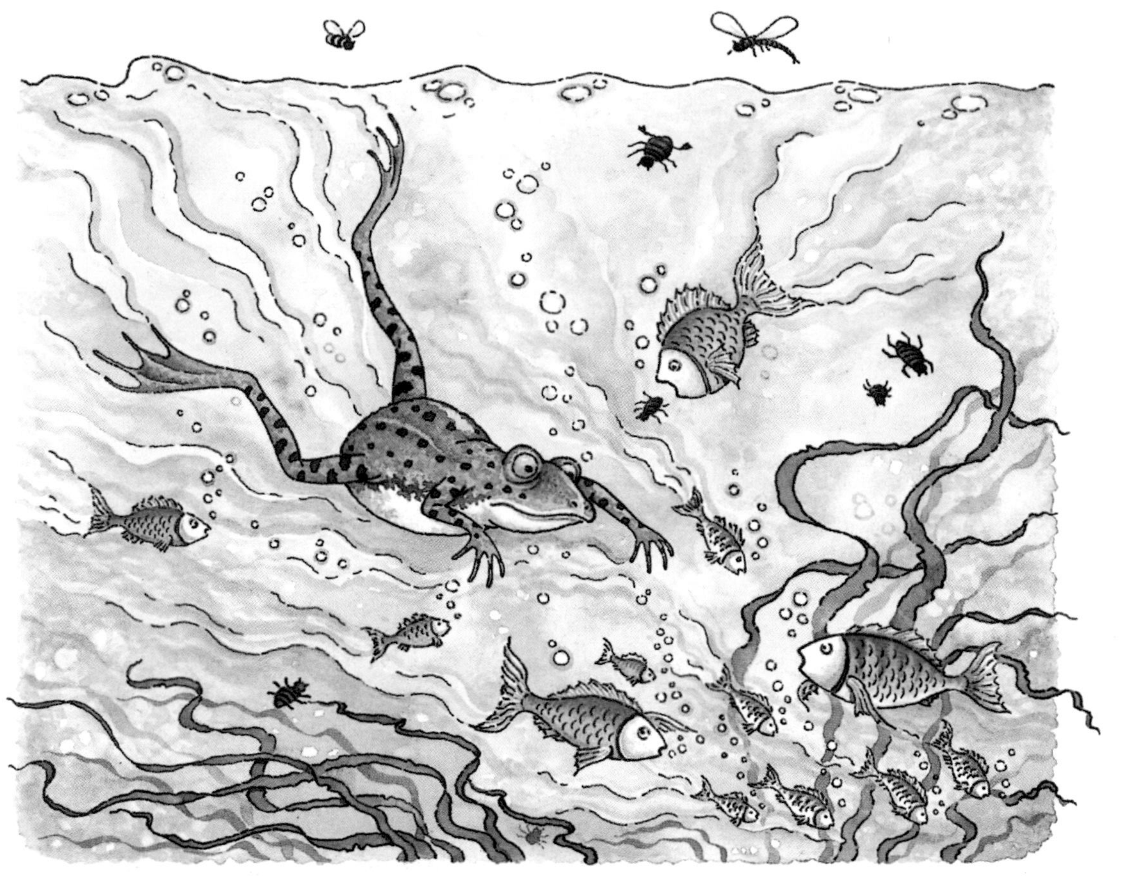

After a long time the frog came swimming up again with the golden ball. Ivy was overjoyed!

The frog threw the ball on to the grass beside Ivy and she picked it up and hugged it. Then she turned and ran off home as fast as she could.

Quickly the frog hopped out of the water.

"Wait for me! Wait for me!" he croaked.

He hopped along trying to catch up but was soon left far behind. Without looking back Ivy kept on running across the fields towards her father's castle.

A week and a day later Ivy had forgotten all about the frog. She was sitting at dinner with the King and all his courtiers when a messenger entered the great hall and announced, "Your Majesty, there is a frog at the door who says that Princess Ivy promised to share her dinner with him."

Ivy looked shocked and her face turned red.

"Is this true, Ivy?" said the King, looking very surprised.

"Well... it is a bit true," said Ivy. Then she told her father what had happened in the big wood and what the frog had asked of her. "I promised him that he could come and live with me," she said, "but I never thought he would follow me all the way home. I don't want to live with a slimy old frog."

The King was a good and honest man who never told a lie and always kept his word. He shook his head and said, "My dear, when a promise is made it must be kept. You must ask the frog to dine with you."

Ivy felt ashamed and reluctantly asked the messenger to show the frog in.

Presently the frog hopped into the great hall and sat by Ivy's chair.

"You promised I could sit beside you," said the frog. Ivy couldn't bear to touch the frog so she picked it up with her napkin and put it on the table. The frog smiled at her and sat beside her plate.

Ivy called for a servant to bring some beetles and pondweed for him but the frog said, “No, I want to eat what you eat, Princess. You promised I could eat from your golden plate and drink from your golden cup.”

The thought of this made Ivy feel quite sick and she didn’t want to eat any more. The frog, however, enjoyed every bite.

When he had finished the frog said to Ivy, "Now I'm tired, please take me to your room."

Ivy turned to the King and said, "Do I have to?" The King looked at her sternly and said, "Yes, you do. The frog helped you when you were in need and you made him a promise."

So Ivy carried the frog to her bedroom, but as she passed her maid she whispered, “Bring a fishtank with a lid to my bedroom, now.”

When the maid brought the fishtank (in which she’d put a stone and some tadpoles to keep the frog company) Ivy quickly popped the frog inside and shut the lid, then she climbed into bed.

"No, no, no," said the frog, jumping up and down, "you promised I could sleep on a silk cushion beside your bed!" And he jumped up and down so much he knocked the lid off the fishtank and hopped out. "If you don't put me on a cushion beside your bed I shall tell the King you do not keep your promises."

Ivy remembered what her father had said. With tears in her eyes she picked up the frog and put him on a silk cushion beside her bed. How unhappy she was. She didn't want to live with a green frog for the rest of her life!

"Now kiss me goodnight," the frog said.

"Oh, how horrible!" thought Ivy, but again, she knew her father would insist. Trying to pretend she was somewhere else, she leaned over, closed her eyes, pursed her lips... and kissed the frog...

Suddenly the room was filled with bright lights and stars! Ivy opened her eyes and couldn't believe what she saw. The frog had disappeared! He had turned into a handsome prince!

"Oh thank you, thank you!" he said. Then he told Ivy how a wicked witch had put a spell on him and turned him into a frog. The spell could only be broken if a beautiful princess would befriend him, eat with him, sleep beside him and kiss him.

The Frog Prince, whose name was Frederick, told Princess Ivy how he had seen her playing with her golden ball in the wood and had fallen in love with her.

Princess Ivy blushed. "We must tell my father what has happened," she said. The King was very surprised when he saw Prince Frederick with Ivy but he was so glad that she was not going to live with a frog.

Princess Ivy and Prince Freddy, as he was better known, became the best of friends and were always together. On sunny days they played in the fields with Princess Ivy's golden ball, or in the wood where Prince Freddy taught Princess Ivy how to swim; and on wet days they played indoors with Prince Freddy's aquarium.

After a year and a day Princess Ivy and Prince Freddy were married. The King was delighted and there were celebrations throughout the land. Within seven years the Princess and Prince had seven children, who were surprisingly good at both swimming and leapfrog, and they all lived happily ever after.